This book belongs to

....

....

EGMONT

Illustrated by Tommy Stubbs

EGMONT
We bring stories to life

First published in Great Britain 2016 by Egmont UK Limited
The Yellow Building 1 Nicholas Road London W 11 4AN

Thomas the Tank Engine & Friends ™

CREATED BY BRITT ALLCROFT

Based on the Railway Series by the Reverend W Awdry
© 2016 Gullane (Thomas) LLC. Thomas the Tank Engine & Friends and
Thomas & Friends are trademarks of Gullane (Thomas) Limited.
Thomas the Tank Engine & Friends and Design is Reg. U.S. Pat. & Tm. Off.
© 2016 HIT Entertainment Limited.

HIT entertainment

ISBN 978 1 4052 8158 4
63482/1
Printed in UK

One sunny day on the Island of Sodor, Thomas the Tank Engine chuffed into Vicarstown Station and saw a shiny new engine. Gordon pulled up next to Thomas and sighed. "That's my brother. They call him the Flying Scotsman."

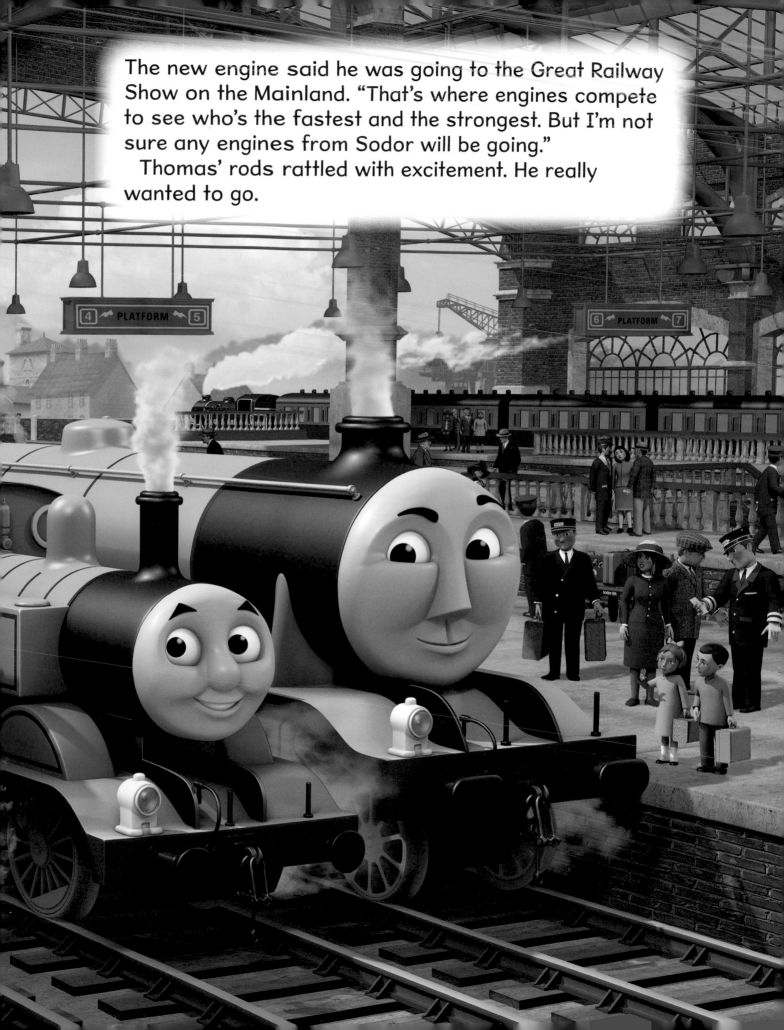

The new engine said he was going to the Great Railway Show on the Mainland. "That's where engines compete to see who's the fastest and the strongest. But I'm not sure any engines from Sodor will be going."

Thomas' rods rattled with excitement. He really wanted to go.

Thomas found The Fat Controller and suggested that an engine from Sodor be upgraded so it could win races at the show.

"That is an excellent idea," The Fat Controller said. "Once he's been streamlined, Gordon will be faster than ever."

Gordon! That was *not* what Thomas had in mind!

The next day, a railway ferry made a very exciting delivery to Brendam Docks. Thomas watched as engines from all over the world rolled ashore.

"Where are you going?" the Dock Manager asked.

"The Great Railway Show," puffed a streamlined Belgian engine.

"That's not here, it's happening on the Mainland," the Manager replied.

"Everybody back on the ship!" shouted an Italian shunter.

The engines jostled and pushed past Thomas as they returned to the ferry.

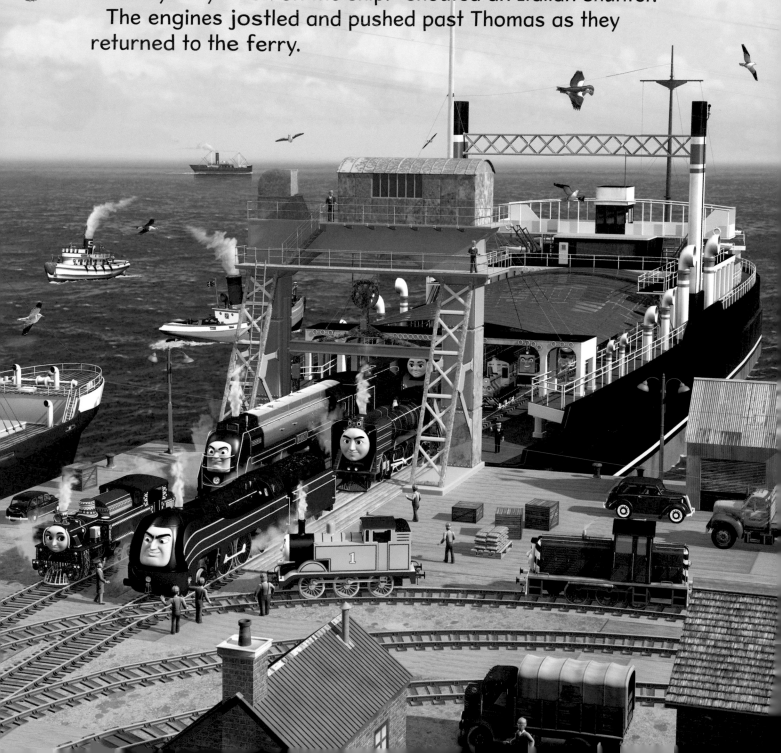

A brightly painted engine named Ashima rushed for the departing ferry — and bumped into Thomas!

"Whoa!" he peeped as he teetered on the edge of the quay.

Dockworkers quickly wrapped a chain around Thomas' coupling hook. With Ashima's help, they pulled him back from the edge.

Ashima apologised for bumping Thomas and asked if there was another way to the Mainland since she'd now missed her ferry.

But Thomas didn't answer. He just chugged away in a huff.

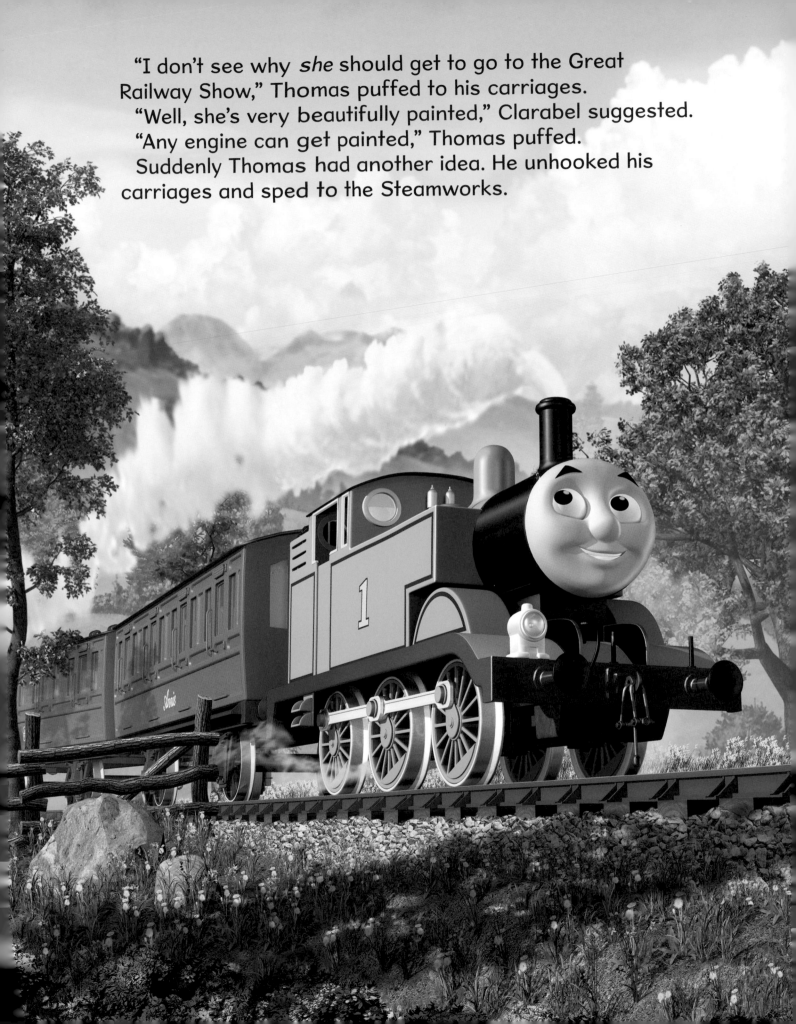

"I don't see why *she* should get to go to the Great Railway Show," Thomas puffed to his carriages.

"Well, she's very beautifully painted," Clarabel suggested.

"Any engine can get painted," Thomas puffed.

Suddenly Thomas had another idea. He unhooked his carriages and sped to the Steamworks.

Thomas told Victor he needed to be repainted. "I was thinking maybe lightning bolts and racing stripes."

But just as Victor went to work, The Fat Controller stopped by to check on Gordon's streamlining. Thomas tried to hide and ended up covered in paint!

Meanwhile, over at the Dieselworks, Diesel had an idea of his own. He wanted to disguise Paxton, Den, and Dart as his trucks and pretend to pull them.

"I'll look like I'm pulling a very heavy train all by myself," he announced with a snicker. "And if The Fat Controller thinks I'm stronger than Henry, he'll take *me* to the Great Railway Show instead."

Later that day, Thomas met Ashima again. She didn't understand why Thomas had wanted to be painted like her.

"You can only be you," she tooted. "Every engine I've ever known was useful and had a job they could do." Ashima asked Thomas if he was good at shunting and sorting trucks.

"Yes," Thomas peeped. And then he had his best idea yet for going to the Great Railway Show. "I'll show The Fat Controller what *I* can do best!"

The next morning Thomas went to Knapford Station to practise his shunting, but the rails were blocked by Diesel's tricky trucks. Thomas decided to move them himself.

"What are you doing?" Diesel hissed. "You'll spoil my trick!"

The disguised diesels started to chug along with Thomas. He was surprised by how easily everything moved — and how quickly!

There was a red signal ahead. Thomas tried
to stop, but the diesels kept pushing because
they couldn't hear the warning bell.
CRASH! Thomas collided with a passing
engine named Norman.

It was the day of the Great Railway Show, and all the engines The Fat Controller had chosen were ready to go. Gordon had been painted and streamlined. He even had a new nameplate: The Shooting Star.

The Fat Controller had wanted Thomas to go for the Shunting Challenge, but now Thomas needed to be repaired after his accident. Percy would go in his place. Thomas tooted goodbye to the engines. He even wished Ashima good luck.

Later that morning, Victor and Kevin discovered that
Gordon's safety valve had never been installed after his
streamlining! Without the valve, Gordon could dangerously
overheat during his race.

Even though his own repairs weren't finished, Thomas
took the valve and steamed across Vicarstown Bridge to
the Mainland.

Thomas reached the Great Railway Show. He eagerly searched the crowds of visiting engines and found Gordon on the starting line of the Great Race.

But Gordon wouldn't listen to Thomas. "Nonsense! The team at the Steamworks is very efficient, and besides, the race is starting *now*!"

A whistle blew, green flags waved, and the engines took off!

Gordon raced along the tracks, passing the other engines. "Shooting Star coming through!" he announced loudly.

But suddenly his face turned red and steam hissed from inside his streamlining.

Gordon's brother, the Flying Scotsman, tried to warn him that something was wrong, but Gordon wouldn't listen . . . until his boiler burst! He sputtered to a stop in a cloud of steam as the other engines sped on.

"Oh, the indignity," he peeped.

Meanwhile, over at the Shunting Challenge, Percy was too scared to enter the competition. He wanted Thomas to compete in his place.

"OK," Thomas peeped. "But I might lose, you know."

But Thomas didn't lose. He chuffed through round after round, pulling tankers and flatbeds into line. He beat **big** engines from Russia, Italy and Brazil.

In the end, there were only two engines left — Thomas and Ashima!

A whistle blew, and the final challenge began.

The two engines steamed back and forth, buffering boxcars into place. Soon their sidings were full, and it was a race to the finish line. But then Thomas noticed an overturned truck on Ashima's track! He sped along to push it out of her way.

Ashima raced to victory.

"Thomas, you let me win," Ashima peeped.

"I know," Thomas replied. "But it wouldn't have been fair. Your track was blocked."

Soon after, everyone gathered for the award ceremony. "We would like to declare *two* winners in the Shunting Challenge," announced a judge. Ashima had won for the fastest time, and Thomas had also won — for helping his competitor.

All the engines whistled and cheered. Even Gordon's brother, the Flying Scotsman, admitted that he was impressed with the engines from Sodor.

The Great Railway Show **START and FINISH** The Great Railway Show

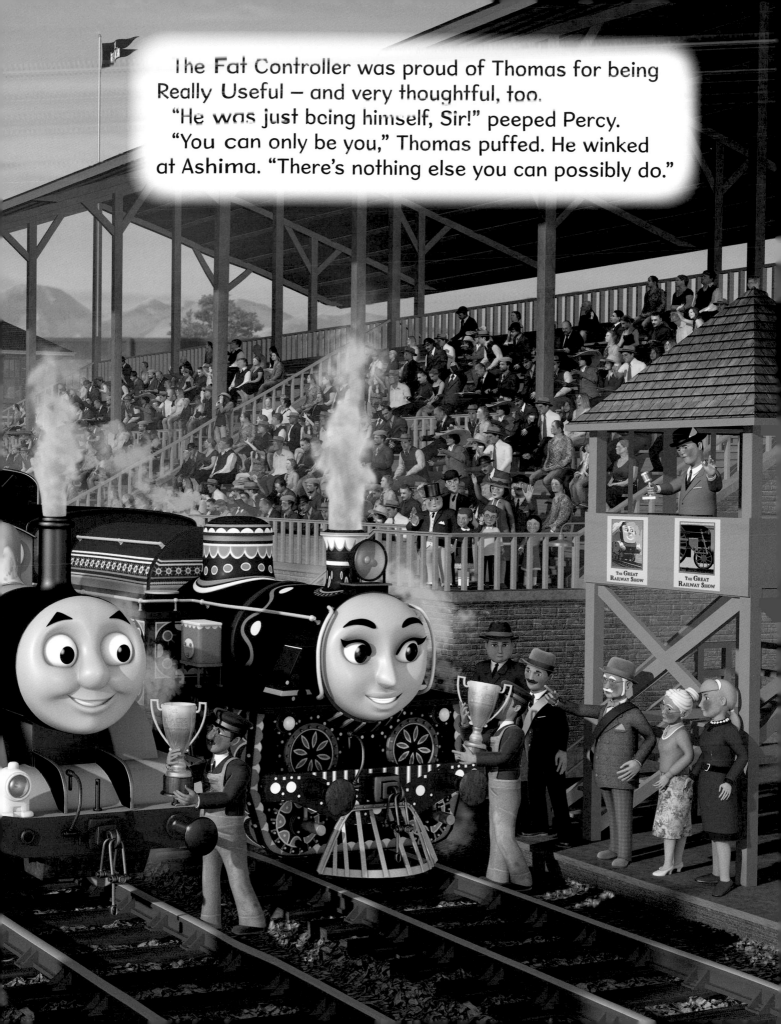

The Fat Controller was proud of Thomas for being Really Useful – and very thoughtful, too.

"He was just being himself, Sir!" peeped Percy.

"You can only be you," Thomas puffed. He winked at Ashima. "There's nothing else you can possibly do."

In the early 1940s, a loving father crafted a small blue wooden engine for his son, Christopher. The stories this father, the **Reverend W Awdry,** made up to accompany the wonderful toy were first published in 1945. Reverend Awdry continued to create new adventures and characters until 1972, when he retired from writing.

Tommy Stubbs has been an illustrator for several decades. Lately, he has been illustrating the newest tales of Thomas and his engine friends, including *Hero of the Rails, Misty Island Rescue, Day of the Diesels, Blue Mountain Mystery* and *King of the Railway*.